Plantain Jane

(Rev. C)

Plantain Jane

Copyright © 2013, 2021 Bernard Dennis Boylan

Third Revised Edition, April 2021

All rights reserved, including the right to reproduce this book, or portions thereof, in any form.

Plantain Jane

(Rev. C)

By:

Bernard D. Boylan

Dedication: My Angel

Preface

Table of Contents

    Section 1: Love's Spontaneity

1. The Neighborhood
2. Plain Jane
3. Sincere Tom
4. The Arts
5. *Walden*
6. Jane's Theological Explanations
7. Pregnancy: a Walk in the Park

    Section 2: Tragedy

8. Jane and a Mid-Wife
9. Dreadful Calls
10. Disabled Widower; Tom Story: *Getting the Kinks Out*
11. A Partial Recovery

    Section 3: Recovery

12. *Colby and Bryan*
13. *Barbara*
14. *Rebuilding*
15. Potpourri of Culture, Writing, and Tears
16. Holidays
17. Story: *Revisions to Mindset*
18. Conclusion
19. The Rising Tide of Optimism; Optimism, 2016

Sources

Dedicated to my "Angel"

Poem, Neil and Father's Day   Bernard D. Boylan

June, 2013

    Jim introduced Tom to a friendly couple,
    Who were renting a house in Noank.
    Neil was a successful businessman,
    They settled at a pond in North Stonington,
    In a home perfect for entertaining, and,
    Long-distance swimming.

    Tom met them on Sundays, after 10 a.m. Mass,
    Their personalities gained many friends,
    A small church fire necessitated,
    Mass in the Round in the center, next door,
    When repairs were completed, Mass moved back,
    Despite protests, the Bishop wouldn't intercede.

    A vibrant splinter group, the Mystic Pilgrims,
    was formed, Neil was the unofficial leader,
    of this bi-monthly prayer group,
    They met at various locales, with different presiders,
    Through the years Tom attended several times,
    But always returned to his conservative base.

    Years later, he got dangerously run-down,
    From too-much work and hiking,
    Not enough sleep, lots of worry, and a lousy diet.
    At a Bible study lecture, Neil and his wife, Pat
    Recognized the signs and began to assist,
    With gifts of cash and good advice.

They enabled him to publish one book and,
Produce a few handsome copies of many others.
Neil advised him to seek better medical help,
And to get more sleep.
When his car was totaled and another needed,
They sent cash for a down payment.

"Also, have some fun with Nat,"
We visited, but didn't comprehend,
The seriousness of Pat's illness,
Tom has reached God three times,
Once was about her, but,
God wouldn't change the course of the Universe.

She died in 2009,
Lonely Neil almost died in a crash.
Then just as he had married Jim years ago,
Now Jim married Neil and Irene in 2012,
A happy second marriage between equals,
Jewish women take better care of their men.

Through the years Neil kept his eyes on Tom,
Calling when he needed advice,
"Friendship has a distinct redemptive power," *The Soloist.*
Sending checks so "his manure pile wouldn't stink,"
Acting as a surrogate father,
Who didn't need fancy shirts, or books by amateurs.

"The simple act of being someone's friend
Can change their brain chemistry and alter the
Functioning of their life." (Quote from *The Soloist*)
So on Father's Day Tom finished this Poem:
Thanks, Dad!

Preface

I'm Bernie from Groton, Connecticut, living in a complex of four-unit buildings. Many of you know me as "the author".

Although I try, my work is certainly not professional or academic, but the storytelling of everyday incidents. In this I've been distinctly unsuccessful.

So in effect, this is my "Apologia." Though most books were amateurish, others were original and almost brilliant. Yet few were read. I served my parents, country and church, paid for my own education, fathered four all-American kids, introduced color copying and computer design to the Mystic area, but failed in business and writing. On the other hand, writing is a hobby that's kept me busy in retirement.

This novella contains fragments of familiar stories, but also contains many new ones, avoiding tales told too often. It brought back memories.

Multiple times I've worked too hard, accumulating a huge sleep-lag. The essence of ideas had to be captured before being lost. Cooperation with neighbors led to earlier bedtimes. My bookcase is overflowing, my health equal to friends, and an "angel" has been charitable. Is steady work the answer to long life? Nobody knows, except that genes control a great deal of longevity unless shortened by bad habits.

I've made a life of my own. Although I can't swing dance any more, I still walk, have lunch with friends, go to cultural events, and occasionally take a friend to dinner. Many intriguing events and people have crossed my path. I hope you find these slivers of retired life interesting.

I wish to thank the wonderful employees and librarians at Groton Public for help, my "angel" for stimulus, and friends for advice.

Reading about the Quakers was stimulating, but make no mistake—I worship as a Catholic, believe in God, and live by "Pascal's Wager—"
>"If I gain, I gain all; If I lose, I lose nothing."
>*The Age of Louis XIIV,* by the Durants

Section 1: Love's Spontaneity

1. The Neighborhood

West Arlington was a quiet hilltop of mostly elderly and middle-aged couples. Gaps between, or behind, ranch houses and three-story tenements were plied with gardens. Finger-like streets stretched up and over the hill and dead-ended at a pond or the sandbanks. Only one part-time business existed, a basement barber. Few children lived here and no playgrounds, but potential play areas abounded: "duck" pond, the forbidden sandbanks, Spectacle pond, trees for climbing and forts, and a long storm drainage ditch alongside "hospital" hill that stretched for a hundred yards to a tiny cat-o-nine tails swamp with willow trees on Spectacle pond.

A childless widow, who could no longer take care of herself, had recently been moved from her second floor apartment to a nursing home. The flat only had to be advertised one day before a young couple drove up, parked alongside the wire link fence, and introduced themselves. The flat wasn't at all luxurious, but it had two bedrooms, a bath, and a large kitchen with a kerosene stove for heating and cooking.

Many neighbors watched as the couple slowly walked around the house with the owner, a second- generation Latvian. They noticed the fence to keep kids in and dogs out, extensive flower and vegetable gardens, blueberry bushes protected by netting, fruit trees, the lack of traffic, the availability of city utilities / services, and quickly nodded Yes! Yes! to the owner.
Neighbors liked what they saw: a quiet young couple riding on the crest of the unknown wave of life.

2. Plain Jane

The owner Jim noticed that the Rinaldi's were conservative, very smart, pleasant, but the wife, Jane, was plain as sin. She was in her first trimester of pregnancy. Tom, her husband, loved being with her, didn't make sarcastic remarks, but did tease by calling her "plantain" or "Plantain Jane." Jim knew he referred to the ubiquitous weed that grew in lawns, "English Plantain," a sturdy, persevering plant with tiny flowers. He assumed they were deeply in love, because no sarcastic response followed. Jim reckoned that Jane was the quiet type, a sturdy woman that would bend not break, and always be cheerful. Her smile made her husband glad and made the marriage worthwhile.

Jane and her younger sister, Barbara, were from a small town in Ohio. Her father was the butcher in the grocery store, and got really busy whenever pig butchering was needed. The boys she met were farmers but like many American women, she didn't want to live on a farm. She wanted to live in a city near people, jobs, and events. Besides, even farm boys wanted pretty girls and she had heard too many taunts about plainness.

Oberlin University looked like an attractive school to study music, especially the flute. But she wasn't allowed to choose. Her father sent her to study business administration at Malone College, a small Quaker school in Canton Ohio. She felt lucky and didn't put up a fight. Many girls never had a chance and wound up marrying into harsh Mennonite or Amish farm families.

Malone had very little social life and few excursions. She studied hard, went to a few events with friends, but couldn't go out alone. When her parents visited, Dad checked her closet for "wild" clothes—she was raised as a Quaker and had to wear plain clothes. The unspoken threat was that she would be pulled out of school and lose this opportunity. So she behaved.

In her senior year, an old friend at Brown University in Providence, R.I., asked Jane to visit on Spring break. By now, her father suffered from senility. Financed by a new credit card, she took three buses and a cab to get to Brown. Students helped find her friend. Jane couldn't believe how wild and free the students were. Clothes and tees of every description barely covered torsos. Were bras out of fashion? Beer cans were everywhere. The campus newspaper reported that a piano had been pushed out a second floor window during a Frat party. Boys flagrantly carried six-packs into the female areas of the dorm. "So this is co-education," she wondered. The big campus event was about to start, a rock concert on the grass of a quad.

The concert was jammed with drunks—a terrible place to find a mate—too many arrogant wise guys. They insulted her plainness and refusal to drink. Then Tom walked in. He had black hair, tan shorts, and a plain white tee without logos. She perked up; was it love at first sight?

He introduced himself. When Tom learned her first name, a nickname immediately came to his mind, "Plantain Jane," a rhyme based on the wildflowers on everyone's lawn.

Tom was a year older. Though short, he appealed to women because of good looks, gentleness, and confidence. He didn't attend college, but was sensible, hardworking, and different from today's crowd. When she met him she would have loved to jump in bed right away, but refused to compromise her principles. Jane gave Tom her friend's phone number, hoping and praying he would understand; when her phone rang, she was so grateful and relieved to hear his voice.

Her parents disapproved of the marriage by a justice of the peace, didn't attend, and never visited. They wanted Jane to marry a Quaker, but she fell in love with Tom and married him despite their tenuous finances.

Jane may have been plain, but she cherished the attention and kidding because she knew from his tone of voice that he loved her. They didn't have money for a honeymoon or trips, the memories of which have sustained many couples during the difficult child-rearing years. It was a shame. After paying the bills together on Sunday nights, little was left. But Jane's Quaker ideas and business administration training enabled her to establish a budget: no chips, crackers, bottled water, exotic juices, or alcohol; just basic American food like Shepherd's pie, beans and franks, or Spaghetti.

If their landlords had extra food, and they deliberately cooked extra, they sent Latvian dishes or vegetables or seafood upstairs. Jim helped because he knew they were on a tight budget—and reliable tenants were hard to find. Jane smiled when he climbed the wooden stairs and lightly knocked; "Sveiki" hello, and "here's something good." He always invited her, afterward, "nak uz legu," come on down.

By noon, the late summer heat in the early 1960s was oppressive and they gathered under the tree. The heat was too much for the window fans. Air conditioners were beginning to appear in a few windows because of lower prices. Exhausted Tom slept through it, but Jane sought relief with Jim's wife, Helene, talking about recipes or sales, while Jim worked in his big gardens. They were pleasant old-fashioned Americans, who knew the value of a buck.

In public, Jane wore presentable but plain clothes, never flashy ones. Tom learned that she did this deliberately because she was a Quaker. He was raised Catholic, yet only occasionally attended Mass. He was curious about all religions. At first he thought all Quakers dressed like William Penn on the Quaker Oats box, or were similar to the Amish or Mennonites. Soon he would learn. He was smarter than his grades would indicate and set about to be a good provider for his Plantain.

Once again, she thought of her family. Jane's sister Barbara was four years younger. After high school she married a farm boy and wrote cursory notes about the difficulty of farm life. She learned how to pickle, how to hang herbs and squash from the basement rafters, how to can, and how to use everything on a butchered pig. Her elderly mother-in-law was helpful because she knew how hard farm life was on a young woman. Apparently, Barbara didn't even have time to play solitaire; no play, just work. Jane understood perfectly the reason for infrequent, self-censored replies and didn't want to embarrass her sister. So she answered by writing about neighbors, nature, New England, and sometimes about Tom. She never asked questions.

Jane's life was easier; she felt guilty but Tom didn't want her to work. He insisted on being the provider. Though he belonged to a union, it was impossible for wages to keep up with inflation. Both management and workers knew textiles were moving south, so contract demands were muted, and only small increases appeared in paychecks. Summer overtime at time and a half was great, but left little time with Jane. He spent time with her on weekends.

Years earlier when Tom dated a blonde bombshell, his cousins taunted him, "You'll be sorry!" He listened and completely understood: beauty is skin deep, usually short-lived, and can't withstand setbacks. On the other hand, while visiting, Tom had sensed the camaraderie between Jane, her sister, and her mother, working together in a tight kitchen. It was so wholesome.

On Sunday, he hailed, "Plantain, come on down to meet your neighbors." She had already met some of them. His new neighbors, especially loud Kenny from across the street, joshed him about his noisy car. Tom promised to replace the muffler by calling with instructions. Jane could drive a loaner and pick him up at the plant.

During the afternoon, three of Jim's brothers arrived, and casually slipped into joking about the old days and his garden. He gave everyone a small bag of tomatoes and a beer. His wife Helene served the best iced coffee Tom ever had. He learned Helene made delicious apple and blueberry pies and she promised to give Jane lessons. Everyone was so good-natured, despite the joking in this mostly male bond. No arguments, only teasing. Their simple competent ways were reminiscent of Jane's parents in Ohio and made her feel right at home. When Tom introduced her as "Plantain Jane," everyone laughed-they knew their plants and liked her smile. That relaxing afternoon was repeated many times.

3. Sincere Tom

Several weekends later, Tom relaxed with a soda under a tree and answered questions about their lives. Everyone listened attentively.

At present, he worked as a screen printer on the twelve-hour second shift in a loft of the ancient granite, ivy-covered mill. Only the lead man and Tom worked this shift. The first shift left detailed notes about the screen numbers and type of cloth to be used. With breaks after each job, the two men lifted the heavy screens, skipped a position, placed the edge of the screen against the "key", swabbed the color back and forth, and skipped to the next position on the extremely long table. After drying, the alternate positions were swabbed. Tom wasn't big to start with, but became more muscular every week.

The only printing still done at the "Print Works" was screen printing. That was because a big facility was required for the long tables and this loft was already available and empty. Buyers from the garment district in the City loved the operation because it was only a short train and taxi ride away.

Tom was a veteran and hired because his boss was a veteran of WWII. Tom served in the Army between wars to do his duty, but didn't consider re-enlistment. Editorials about the "domino theory" and South Vietnam began to appear: reputable officials swore that one by one all the countries in Southeast Asia would fall. War was on the horizon. Tom had inactive reserve duty remaining so on Sundays he read carefully.

Young veterans played poker in a nearby VFW. It was harmless gambling and bantering and it let the guys blow off steam. Tom refused to play because weekends were special—he didn't want to leave Jane all alone. Besides he was lousy at poker or card counting. When a fellow high school veteran asked if he wanted to go hunting for a week up north, Tom refused. He had been so frozen for weeks on winter maneuvers that he never wanted to be cold again. Years later, he read between the lines of a history book and understood the unpublicized reason why a GI walked day and night during the Battle of the Bulge—the guy was afraid that frostbite would cause a loss of toes because of the lousy Army boots.

After they returned from the movies on Saturday nights, Tom gently gathered Jane in his arms and began sweet-talking her. They both loved the foreplay and smooching and love- making. Afterward, they slept in one another's arms.

Tom loved to tease, especially his new neighbor Kenny, who was a tinsmith by trade and a jack-of-all-trades. Kenny married late in life, remodeled his home several times, but only had one child from the coupling. Tom knew it was a sore spot and avoided it. Everything else was fair play. The men kidded one another fiercely.

Jim and Kenny had a daily dispute: who had the most acreage? Who was "the King of West Arlington?"

Both had large holdings. Kenny even went to Town hall to figure it out.

Next day, Jim asked, "What did you find out?"

Kenny was sheepish, "You win by half a lot," at first, they laughed together and then roared—two good friends.

Jim grew about everything possible in New England, except potatoes. Tom was impressed and told Jane that someday he might have a garden: smaller but concentrating on the most expensive vegetables, like Jim.

Jane and Tom were raised in different religions, so they alternated attendance. The first time Tom attended a Quaker service; he sat quietly on a bench in a squared circle with the others for thirty minutes and whispered to the next guy, "When does the service begin?"

"When the worship ends, the service will begin."

Tom prayed for long periods at St. Mary's when his parents died, but was usually physically exhausted on weekends from his twelve-hour shift, and almost a stranger at church. And that's how good-natured Fr. Nardillo greeted him after Mass, "Hello, stranger!"

Tom was curious. Since Jane was from a mid-west town that was a hot box of religions, after Mass, she patiently explained the differences between Mennonites, Amish, and Quakers.

"Mennonites were an Anabaptist sect from Germany that emphasized God as the audience, not the congregation. Services were led by a worship leader, a minister, and witnesses from believers. A Cappella singing has now been supplemented by instruments and a song leader. Mennonites emphasized reading the bible but allowed time for reflection. No titles were used. Participation was broad."

"The Amish split off from other sects in Germany and held services in homes, basements, shops, and barns for financial reasons, and because of their emphasis on believers as the true church. The three-hour services had singing, prayer, and the preaching of two sermons, one short and one long. Males led the bi-monthly services with men sitting on one side and women the other. Housewives had to tidy homes and prepared the standard menu of an after-church meal. Others helped. They ate in shifts with the elderly first and kids last. If a family broke off from the Amish, they usually joined the Mennonites.

Quakers aren't similar to the Amish or Mennonites. They split from the established Church of England when George Fox, the founder, started preaching in 1647. At first, gray clothes, large hats, and bonnets were worn, like William Penn, but are no longer used. They also stood out by saying, 'thee and thou'.

The Quaker philosophy was quiet contemplation and stewardship, urging a shedding of "...cumber until the center is reached, where our spirit makes us whole."

Quakerism was born in England in the 1650s, a time when English society was rigidly stratified by social class. The Quakers, however, believed that the Light of God shone equally in all people, so they refused to bow, use honorific titles, or doff their hats.

"Tell me about William Penn," Tom asked, "I see him every day on the cereal box."
Jane began, "He was a philosopher and founder of Pennsylvania, who advocated democracy, religious freedom, and good relations with Native Americans. He planned and developed Philadelphia, supported colonial unity, and his imprint is found in our Constitution. His convictions came from early Christianity. His book, *No Cross, No Crown,* is a religious classic."

"At 15, a Quaker missionary inspired Penn. Oxford expelled him for rebelling against forced worship. Travel and study in France improved his manners, dress, and he adopted free will. At 22, he officially became a Quaker. Here's the distinction: the Quakers refused to bow, remove hats, pay tithes, or make oaths. God communicated to each directly. Penn was an ally of George Fox, the founder, and helped to establish Quakerism. When he traveled to Germany, he proposed mass emigration. King Charles of England repaid debts to his dad by granting him Pennsylvania. He became a practical promoter, planner, and governor for his "Holy Experiment." Quakers and minorities were attracted. His laws were progressive and puritanical. The idea of document amendments was developed by him.

Sadly, his business manager embezzled thousands and swindled ownership from him. Penn died penniless after two strokes. That cereal logo is no longer claimed to be him.

Though not popular, Quakerism had admirable qualities: avoid fanciness in dress, speech, and possessions because Jesus taught "love thy neighbor as thyself." The testimony is expressed in the plain walls and simple functional furniture in meeting houses. Friends dress in plainer versions of current fashion; they no longer look like William Penn.

In speech, Quaker plainness fosters honesty, no class distinctions, an avoidance of paganism, speaking the truth, the use of verbal affirmation for deals, fixed prices without haggling, no honorific titles, no swearing oaths, and no ornate grave monuments.

The following quote is taken from *Plain Living* by C. Whitmire:

"I had a memorable Quaker friend named Ed Morgenroth who, during his eighty-plus years of life, was a vital force in early childhood education, prison reform, and interfaith relationships. In his elder years Morgen would exclaim, not infrequently, "I like simple living, and a lot of it!" In his exclamation are qualities of freedom, playfulness, and joie de vivre that we cannot possibly get from the costly commercial "entertainments" with which we are surrounded, qualities that come only from appreciating the elemental gift of life."

4. The Arts

Tom's boss said the backlog of jobs was dropping and by fall they would return to eight-hour shifts. That was a relief—He wanted to be with Jane and take her to more of the area's cultural events. His folks had never been interested in the arts, only movies at a local theatre. It was a big hole in his education. When Plantain explained, his mind siphoned energy, knowledge and excitement from her brain into that same lobe of his brain and made him eager for the next weekend. They gathered all the pamphlets and advertisements, made a list of the dates, the cost, and chose events.

In the fall, they attended a symphony; Mussorgsky's *Pictures at an Exhibition* was featured. It was fantastic and Tom loved it. When he heard the downward spiral and crescendo of "The Great Gate of Kiev," Tom felt his mind become the music; everything else was blotted out. Although emotionally drained, he wanted it to go on forever.

Jane taught, "It's important to learn different nationalistic styles and periods in order to place them in context." She liked Russian music the best. They enjoyed performances together, made friends with the next young couple, and decided to attend a few more concerts.

Jane was a good teacher, who only fed him enough to grasp. They didn't agree on art—he liked realists like Norman Rockwell and the Wyeths, and surprisingly, she, modern art, especially Picasso, Matisse and Kandinsky. "After our children are born, we'll go to the City to see the museums." When decorating with prints, they compromised on styles—after all, Jane said, "good art is good art, regardless of its age."

Monthly poetry sessions were held on Fridays but Tom worked. However, their new friends invited them to attend a Sunday afternoon reading in a private salon that resembled a European salon with art, piano music, poetry, and conversation. They arrived early, intending to leave early, too, but were so enraptured they stayed for the entire session. Jane felt like George Sand, listening to poetry with Chopin's background music. The salon owners had good taste with museum quality pieces. But due to Plantain's pregnancy, they took a rain check on wine and thanked their friends and the hosts. "Wasn't everything beautiful?" Tom asked Plantain. "Yes, but in the future," Jane remarked, "We'll avoid impulsive purchasing—it's cumber!"

On other weekends they heard string quartets playing the music of Bach, who was touted as "great" and "the father." However, except for *Air on a G-String, The Well-Tempered Clavier,* and the *Brandenburg Concertos,* Tom disliked the drone of his work. So they usually avoided string quartets. Later he learned that Bach restrained from experimenting too far ahead of the culture of the times.

Jane rarely complained, but did so when a summer outdoor art festival in Wickford extended for way too many blocks and hours on a blazing hot humid day.

5. *Walden*

Several times, Tom expressed interest in a bigger, modern house. So Jane introduced him to an American classic, *Walden,* by Henry David Thoreau. "It will be a revelation," she said.

"*Walden* was written by a renegade from society. It's brilliant but difficult to read because of poor editing, too many references to classical mythology, bad poems, and too many themes: simple living, nature, independence, social experimenting, spiritual discovery, satire, self- reliance, and more. He used many literary techniques and recorded his experiences and reflections while living for two years in a cabin on Walden Pond in Concord, Massachusetts. He wrote two books: *A Week on the Concord and Merrimack Rivers*, and *Walden,* which compressed two years into a single year. He climbed Mt. Katahdin and visited Cape Cod, but saved these experiences for separate essays and a posthumous book, *The Maine Woods* and *Cape Cod.*

Walden was available at the library. A librarian said that no one exemplified the simple life better than Thoreau. At 27, he built a shack on a woodlot on Walden Pond, a mile from the village, and earned a simple living by his own hands. (However, his mom did the laundry and sisters brought food on weekends.) "It was a period of immense personal growth for Henry, during which he struggled ...with the question ... of how little (wealth) a person needs to live well and be free."

The book is unclassifiable: part memoir, part nature, part simple living, and a critique of materialistic culture. The industrial revolution was in full swing, led by water power and the railroads, sparking desire for splendid homes and furnishings. Readers see themselves targeted by *Walden*. However, the book is a reminder that simpler, freer ways exist—we really don't have to live lives of "quiet desperation."

Henry wrote:

"I wish to suggest that a man may be very industrious and yet not spend his time well. There is no more fatal blunderer than he who consumes...his life getting his living."

"Our life is frittered away by detail—Simplify! Simplify! Simplify! I say let your affairs be as two or three and not a hundred or a thousand; instead of a million count half a dozen and keep your account on your thumbnail."

Jane explained, "Simplicity of living was Thoreau's path to genuine freedom. He didn't need 'things' or 'stuff'. He practiced self-discipline and didn't waste his time.

Thoreau wrote, 'My greatest skill has been to want but little.' This lesson is profound—by revising our thinking, we can live a simpler, freer life.

Tom learned phrases in *Walden* that stayed with him for a lifetime. Henry's ideas were cogent and logical. When he explained that he wouldn't know how to spend great wealth, Tom agreed.

Many, many ideas and themes were presented. Henry put his all into this, the work of a lifetime. Tom promised himself to read this masterpiece again.

6. Jane's Theological Explanations

Raised in a Quaker home, Jane was taught that a person's spiritual life and character were more important than their possessions or wealth. Her folks believed that money and time should be used to make life better for others. They were witnesses that a person ought to have a simple life to focus on what is most important, and play down the unimportant.

C. Whitmire wrote in *Plain Living*:
"Plain living is a form of inward simplicity that leads us to listen for the "still, small voice" of God's claim upon our lives. It is both a spiritual lens and a discipline of holy obedience. This way of living simplifies our lives because when we focus our energies on what we discern by listening within, we are able to release the extraneous activities and possessions that clutter our path."

"But when I walked into the meeting for worship on oak floor, boards that glowed with the patina of age; when I sat on one of the simple wooden benches arranged in a squared circle at the heart of a century-old stone barn; when I settled into the silence with thirty or forty people, a silence that flowed on for an hour or so, rippled only occasionally by soulful speech; and when, as never before, I felt God's presence in the sunlight that came through the window and fell on the floor at my feet—then, what passed through me time and again was the peace that passes all understanding."

Tom and Jane often discussed theology on Saturday nights. Quaker upbringing enabled Jane to distill the essence of religions for her husband. Tom confirmed that laymen who participated in Catholic services were mostly wealthy. Jane detested the idolatry of statues, but strangely liked the repetition of the rosary and examples of advent chanting. She particularly liked the representations on the walls of the Stations of the Cross, and asked "Is it possible that they are the earliest historical presentation of Jesus' crucifixion?" Years later, Tom learned that the Stations originated in the Middle Ages.

Jane said Buddhist services were too long. The forty-five minutes of chanting in Sanskrit was followed by an hour of instructions. Five times daily, Muslims are called to pray toward Mecca; arrows were painted on floors. This focus on directions was too much. The multiplicity of Hindu gods was staggering. Chinese prophets, such as Lao Tzu, were fixated on ancestor worship.

"Plantain: enough! I'm turning off the light. You should be a minister. Do the Quakers have ministers?"

"No, they appoint members who take turns."

On the next day, attendance was low at St. Mary's. The reason was the annual Bishop's Appeal; Because of zealous fundraising, many men avoided solicitation and wouldn't provide addresses. Slides of numerous Diocesan charities were shown. Jane was amazed at how many charities existed and how much money for them was required in this small state.

Tom acknowledged to his wife that they couldn't donate.

"All joy arises from a sense of being,
while the main emphasis in our society is on having…"

Damaris Parker-Rhodes, 1985

7. Pregnancy: A Walk in the Park

Except for more trips to the bathroom, tiredness, and size, Tom only noticed a slow change in Jane. The meals and conversation were good. She often placed his hand on her belly to feel the baby's movements.

In early fall, Jane said, "I feel like getting some fresh air. Let's walk to Goddard Park again." Tom was gentler than usual, because he knew it was his duty to help her, and quickly shut off the TV. "Let's go." He helped her down the long steep staircase and into the car.

Sunday afternoon traffic was light, but the parking lot at the State park was jammed. They waited for an open slot near the entrance and the trail. It seemed like every representative of the population was there on one of the last good days of fall: elderly, boy scouts on bikes, joggers, young females, immigrant fisherman, individuals, couples, and dogs of every breed.

Jane walked slowly with Tom. They stopped to chat with young couples about babies and due dates. Owners of leashed dogs happily talked about the characteristics of their breed. The dogs were all friendly. Tom remarked, "I've never seen a nasty one out here." They rested several times.

As they approached the Bay, coastal vegetation took over. A few wrinkled (beach) roses, grew near the water. Their large colorful five-petaled white or pink blossoms and deep green foliage brightened the fall landscape of cedars, white groundsel shrubs, tall tan phragmites reeds, vibrant purple asters, and the plump black berries of Japanese honeysuckle.

A young couple saw that Jane was pregnant and gave up their seats on a bench. Sunday walks have always been a wonderful tradition of exercise and conversation and today it continued. As usual, they marveled over the view. Tom had bonded so close to Plantain, so thoroughly meshed in conversation, that he wasn't alarmed when his sweetheart teased, "At home, I'm going to tell you something I've decided."

Tom was curious. But Plantain was a smart college grad, and would ask other women if a problem arose. The walk back took much longer with many breaks. At home loud Kenny yelled across the road from his green acres, "Where have you been? I thought you had the baby" He had grown up with chums and now was employed by them. Kenny's wife was a real tough nut who never walked with him. She was an Italian Protestant in this tolerant neighborhood. There was little discussion of religion, sex, or politics here. It was a semi-religious, egalitarian haven for agnostics. Roger Williams, the dissenter who founded Rhode Island, would have been proud.

Jane was very tired but cuddled on the couch with Tom. He patted her tummy.

"I'm an old-fashioned girl with old-fashioned habits. I've been talking with Lucy down the street and decided to have an old-fashioned delivery like my ancestors. I'm going to hire her as my mid-wife."

At first, Tom hesitated. But what could a young male know about mid-wifery? He didn't want to start an argument, and agreed, "It's your body and decision; if you've investigated, go ahead."

Section 2: Tragedy

8. Jane and a Mid-Wife

Lucy Huld was a strong, tall, childless housewife, whose husband had a good job. They lived in a disorderly two-story house at the end of the street. She looked for a part-time job that was interesting yet paid well. Lucy tried different occupations: library clerk, portrait painting, and school bus driver, until stumbling on the ancient tradition of mid-wives. A tiny percentage of women dreaded the old horror stories of hospitals during child birthing and wanted home deliveries. But most simply lacked insurance and money.

Lucy took classes and passed the exam. Her first patients were routine and she became confident. When she heard about Jane's pregnancy, although lacking experience or emergency facilities or medicine, she enticed Jane to hire her—after all, they lived on the same street and Jane would save lots of money.

When Jane told Tom her decision, "Lucy is going to be the mid-wife for my baby's delivery." Tom asked, "Does she have a license—is she legit?"

"Yes," said Jane, "Rhode Island has permitted mid-wives for about a hundred years."

***

Tom didn't eat after work—it interfered with sleeping. He woke in midafternoon to the aroma of a big meal before heading off to work. Jane was proud of her hard-working husband, who seldom complained. But today there was little time to question or observe her. He grabbed a full lunch pail loaded with goodies and rushed off.

On rainy weekends, like many naive couples, they tried to figure out how to buy a house. Before work, he called bankers. Tom hated to discourage Plantain, but a house in a good neighborhood was unattainable with his modest income and meager savings.

Jane was trying to help: "a mid-wife costs thousands of dollars less than a hospital and doctors," — clinching the discussion.

***

In later years, Tom tortured himself by reading medical journals and bulletins.
Childbirth is the sixth most common cause of death among American women in her age bracket; about 15 deaths per 100,000. Why is it such an ordeal? Compared to other primates, infants are undeveloped because of the "obstetrical dilemma:" women's hips aren't big enough for the baby's head. Other reasons are called the "metabolic hypothesis: "the use of too much energy during the last trimester makes women susceptible to disease. Then too much labor is required for the baby's head. Now, better nutrition means fewer cases of rickets, which causes bone deformities. The death rate also dropped with Sulfa antibiotics and cleanliness.

One-percent of U.S. women choose home delivery, "trusting their bodies to good old Mother Nature." But doctors say Nature will kill you and intuition is just ignorance, with three times as many deaths among newborns. Whereas hospitals have emergency treatment and medicines if problems arise.

Preeclampsia is the most common complication: blood pressure rises suddenly and swelling occurs. Untreated it leads to eclampsia: convulsions, coma, and death. About five percent of pregnancies are affected. It involves blood vessels in the placenta but the cause is unknown: genetic, traffic pollution, organ damage, or immune system failure.

Early signs are high blood pressure and protein in the urine; then, fluid retention which normally occurs but now is sudden and severe; blurry vision; intense headache; malaise; short breathe; pain below the right ribs; rapid weight gain; vomiting; decrease in urine; decrease in blood platelets; impaired liver, and growth restriction in the fetus.

Risk factors include the first pregnancy; a long gap between pregnancies; a new father; family history; age; and other illnesses like diabetes. A diagnosis is reached by hypertension and protein in urine. The mother is at risk of stroke, seizures, and severe bleeding until her blood pressure comes down. Bed rest, the early inducement of labor, or a Caesarian is common. If untreated, a risk exists of coma, brain damage, and dying.

9. Dreadful Calls

At the Print Works, it was unusual to get any calls at night. The first ring on the company phone came from Lucy before 10 pm. She was concerned, "Your wife is having terrible labor-she wants to see you."

"I'll stop what I'm doing and be home, soon."

Just as he was leaving, ten minutes later, the second call came. Lucy was excited. "I called rescue to take Jane to R.I. Hospital; She's bleeding uncontrollably. You better call to give your permission for treatment."

As he entered the hallway, almost immediately, the phone rang for the third time; his boss answered, and called him back. "Tom, it's for you and it's important."

"This is Dr. Winthrop from rescue. Are you Tom Rinaldi?"

"Yes."

"Your wife is critical! Can we have your permission to treat her?"

"Yes, I'm on the way." Traffic was light and he ran red lights, but it was a long drive and took fifteen minutes to drive from Cranston to the emergency room in Providence. By instinct, Tom found the doctor, but it was too late—

He squeezed Plantain's cold hand, kissed her cheek, and closed and kissed each eyelid.

The doctor was cold and terribly curt: "She died in the ambulance before reaching the hospital. Your daughter died, too."

Tom sobbed so violently that he was given a sedative. "My Plantain; My Plantain!" he cried over and over. He would remember this terrible moment forever and wouldn't let it go.

The doctor prevented him from driving—"Someone else will have to take you home." Tom didn't have Kenny's number so the nurse called a cab. At home

Jim was waiting: "Lucy called. She said you might need help." But Jim had to stop asking questions because Tom became agitated and couldn't control his emotions. Even with medication, they never came under control. They had always been there, hidden, and now exposed; Tom was overwhelmed by emotion.

Later that night, he was still sobbing, as thoughts of his beloved wife ran through his mind, "Her time was up; her time was up! Plantain! My Plantain!"

10. Disabled Widower; Tom

In less than an hour, Tom Rinaldi had lost his wife and daughter. He berated himself, "Why didn't I seek advice, beforehand? Why was I trying to save money? Why didn't I insist that she go to an obstetrician? Why did it take Lucy so long to call for help?"

He had suffered a total loss, a crippling and disabling loss.

No services were held. She was buried in a private cemetery in Ohio with a small white marker.

Jane's parents were nearly speechless; they must have blamed him for the tragedy. But Jane's sister Barbara commiserated with him. Her clothes were plain but framed a pretty dignified smile. Barbara remembered the pleasant words about Tom in the letters from Jane. She had his address and promised to write occasionally. When Tom asked about the bruise on her face, embarrassed, she replied, "I fell in the kitchen."

When another visit led to excessive grief again, a professional advised him to stop visiting.

Every time he walked to the shore, he thought of his wife, "as plain as sin," but so happy and cheerful with him, until the end.

Kenny came over to Tom's apartment to offer condolence; no wisecracks, today, just sorrow over his friend's bad luck. When Tom suggested that Jane's time was up, Kenny agreed and told Tom a strange, but similar story:

"Before I married, I met a Dutch woman named Beatrice, who immigrated after the War. She married another Dutch émigré. Years later, I bumped into her. She had lost her husband to a stroke. He was young, strong, and weighed less than me."

"What happened?" Tom asked.

"She didn't know; maybe his time was up? Beatrice worked as a substitute teacher, raised her daughters, and became very good at crafts to occupy her time. Sometimes she labored for days on calligraphy for wedding announcements. She never found anyone else and last year, died within five days of a quick illness. She never got over her husband's death; maybe her own time was up?

Tom remembered a West German incident. "One night before curfew, a drunken G. I. raced to catch the last stassenbahn to the kaserne. He caught up to it and pulled himself up to the sliding door. A German opened the door and swiveled the American inside, just before a narrow underpass that would have crushed him. Maybe, it wasn't his time to go,"

Kenny paused and then guessed, "Was that you?"

"Yes."

Tom looked so sad that Kenny ended the conversation, "My wife said not to stay long. Call if you need anything."

***

Tom's family told him to wait a decent interval before dating again. Although they said he was still attractive to women, he had had enough-He knew Plantain couldn't be matched and he couldn't take another loss. His candles and prayers would eventually reunite them in heaven. He prayed for hours in empty churches.

Jim alerted Tom's sister about his irrational behavior and she tried to force a visit to a psychiatrist—at first, he refused, becoming as silent as wind whispering at sundown through the wild cherry trees at the Park. He was grateful to Jim, but by the third month after Jane's death, he had to move—too many memories. He asked Kenny, who found a quiet small cabin near the Bay that was winterized. In June, tourists would rent it.

He received calls but no visits. A psychiatrist doubled the dosage of his medicine; his lawyer obtained forms and filed for mental disability for Tom, whose emotions had made him unsuitable for work. Every Christmas he wrote a long letter to her folks until they passed away. The letters were always about Plantain, even though writing wracked him. He kept a journal to aid recovery and often added entries in his letters of sights along the shore that she liked: the long-necked snowy egrets, the white clumps of groundsel shrubs, the multiple wands of goldenrod, the purple asters. So many memories came that tears formed.

He wrote a letter to Jane's sister Barbara in Ohio, but never received a reply.
In June, Tom tried to make a fresh start by making another move; this time to a senior complex in Southeastern Connecticut. But daily walking along the coast only partially revived his personality. Tom reworked a story, *Getting the Kinks Out,* that he and Plantain had written. It offered solace to his emotions.

Story: Getting the Kinks Out

A violent February storm stopped abruptly, initiating a month and a half drought. In March, Tom hiked with the AMC for six miles on the "Narragansett Trail" in Voluntown, CT. They followed the blue-blazes for three hours, including rest breaks. During the preceding week, the weather was windy and cool, but today was warm with a light breeze. So as the temperature climbed, jackets found packs. Visibility from hilltops was the best of the year.

Woodland life was quickening. For the next eight weeks, the forest would pulsate with renewal, On today's hike, wet areas displayed March's only wildflower, skunk cabbage, At other spots, the hikers saw club moss; spongy layers of oak leaves and flattened evergreen Christmas fern; Dark-colored "mourning cloak" butterflies "sailed" the trail; in the forest understory, evergreen mountain laurel thrived; Wood frogs in distant vernal pools quacked louder than ducks.

The trodden dry-leaf path led between bare trees, over small hills, followed gravel roads, and traced a wildly curving brook. Here and there, tree trunks were decomposing. During the February storm, strong gusts toppled a massive white oak. Heavy winter rains had saturated the ground, making the uprooting that much easier. The crash brought to mind the philosophical riddle of Bishop George Berkeley: "If a tree falls in the forest and no one's there to hear it, does it make a sound?"

He believed that reality existed only in the mind of the perceiver: "To be is to be perceived."
The eastern part of the hike followed a picture-perfect, twisting New England creek. Overflowing water levels had dropped fast, exposing sand flats with deer and coyote tracks.

There's nothing like a rejuvenating spring hike: fresh air, friendly companions, and exercise to loosen the winter kinks, boost your spirits, and stimulate your mind.

During the late-winter, Tom heard so many groans from malcontents that it sounded like déjà vu of T.S. Eliot's *The Waste Land*! There was a simple, robust antidote for winter's blahs: Walk the land! Feel the surprising strength of the soaring sun. See last fall's twirled horizontal beech leaves, See the increasing number of adults exercising along the roads, Talk to neighbors raking the last leaves or mulching around shrubs, Crocus and daffodils were blooming and the flaring forsythia was next.

There was no finer place to walk than the rustic roads, new growth woods, hills, beaches and rocky seashore, or the hills, of southern New England. Exercise unlocks everything else. Walking is a best exercise; and along with extensive reading, slows the aging process. To walk under the foliage in North Stonington village, view nearby Fishers Island, sailboats tacking off St. Edmund's on Enders Island, great blue herons gliding past, walking at Bluff Point in Groton; or hiking with the AMC in Eastern Connecticut, provides memories.

Eliot's *The Waste Land* opened ominously, "April is the cruelest month, breeding Lilacs out of the dead land"

In *Walking,* Thoreau wrote, "I believe in the forest, and in the meadow, and in the night in which the corn grows." The Indians possessed the same awe-stricken view of creation as Thoreau, but it's buried by advertising for "things," and adoration of America's gladiators and sex dreams. The primordial sense of God's universe has atrophied from civilization's onslaughts.

To improve attitudes, the winter-weary "wasteland" of New England needs a better catch phrase for spring: One more gracious than T.S. Eliot's; more positive than "March comes in like a lion;" and with more élan than "Beware the Ides of March!" On Friday, during the "Stations of the Cross," part of a slogan came to Tom. Afterward, while walking on the block circle outside the chapel, the remainder fell into place:

"Walk the land to sing a new song!"

11. A Partial Recovery

Tom found that "Plantain" and Thoreau's plain living wasn't simple. It's a lifelong series of decisions to reduce expensive extraneous habits and accomplish simple living. Getting rid of "cumber," the clutter that hinders our approach to God is essential. This basic everyday Quaker philosophy satisfies and rejuvenates.

Plain living, plus allowing sufficient time for contemplation, seemed to satisfy Tom, but his sister insisted he needed help because his emotions stood out starkly. When asked, a neurologist provided a good recommendation. Lab tests for mental problems don't exist. It's up to the psychiatrist to correctly interpret answers to questions before a diagnosis is formed and medicines prescribed. The slow procedure took months.

His apartment was livable, pleasant, and a starting point for nearby excursions. It wasn't long before he realized plain living was great. His composure and problem solving improved.

Tom remembered Thoreau's advice, but recognized that most aspects of simplicity didn't fit modern life. He had no desire to be homeless, to live on the far margins of society because he had had a full taste of all-weather living in the Army. But he knew that a conducive, simple life was attainable on his limited income. So one by one, using Plantain's system, he selected items and services which could be reduced in cost or volume, or eliminated and used the extra for cultural events.

Thoreau found solitary life fulfilling:

"You think that I am ... withdrawing from men, but in my solitude I have woven for myself a silken web or chrysalis, and nymph-like, shall ere long burst forth a more perfect creature, fitted for a higher society."

Journal, February, 1857

"I have lately got back to that glorious society called Solitude."
> *Letter to H. Blake, 1859*

"I am not alone if I stand by myself."
> *A week on the Concord...*

"Men frequently say to me, "I should think you would feel lonesome down there, and want to be nearer to folks, rainy and snowy days and nights especially… What sort of space is that which separates a man from his fellows and makes him solitary? I have found that no exception of legs can bring two minds much nearer to one another."
> *Walden*

Although Thoreau had raved about solitude, Tom found his own approach. He struck a balance between solitude, rest, exercise, and social life. He knew the balance was different in each stage of life. Tom lived "deliberately," "fronting only the essential facts of life."

Section 3: Recovery

12. Colby and Bryan

Soon after moving, Tom met Colby, who lived in the same complex. She inquired if he walked? They agreed to walk three-times weekly. It was too good to be true—it was hard to find a walking partner. Their initial conversations warned Tom that it wasn't a compatible match. So he avoided contact, and she turned into a nuisance.

Still, the lack of a partner irked him and he had to work his way through the chagrin. At lunch, friends chortled, "There's plenty of fish in the sea." They tried to recover his joy.

But his friend Bryan entertained him with an old Irish joke:

"Teddy, m'boy, do y' realize y're approach in' the fortieth year o' your birth and y're still a bachelor?"

"Ay, realize it I do."

"But Teddy—in all them years, did y'not once think of tyin' the connubial knot?"

"Ay, many toymes," said Teddy. "An that's why I stayed single."

His friend Bryan snickered at Milton Berle's joke book; Tom only smiled, his friend meant well.
"A Bachelor wants a girl in his arms, not on his hands."
"He who hesitates is lost—unless he's a bachelor."
"A bachelor is a man who's crazy to get married, and he knows it."

Bryan went on,
"A bachelor is a man who believes in life, liberty and the happiness of pursuit."

The kernel of wisdom behind these jokes kept ruminating in Tom's mind. He had gone through the agony of losing Plantain, and it smashed his emotions. Why did he want to go through it again? Maybe he was lucky, now, to be untethered!

What made Tom think he could support a wife, or a companion? Bryan was a reliable friend with good common sense, who was trying to help. Tom finally admitted the truth to himself: he was bachelor material and happier single. He couldn't afford and didn't require expensive relationships. He counted his blessings.

13. Barbara

In the spring of 1997, Jim, his former landlord called, "What's your current address? I've got a letter from Ohio for you."

Tom picked it up right away. It was from Barbara, Plantain's younger sister. He remembered her as pleasant, but trapped in the never-ending toil of a small farm in a small town. The letter was sent on the stationary of a shelter for battered women and children.

Barbara's husband became tyrannical after a series of bad harvests, causing bills to pile up. He walloped the twins for playing instead of working and when she protected them, he beat her up. The hospital sent her to the agency and the police placed a restraining order on her husband. But her arm was broken and she couldn't function. She didn't have any money. All parents and close relatives were dead. Barbara and the twins needed to be sheltered and a place to recuperate. Jane had always stressed that Tom was gentle, generous, and considerate. Would he be willing to shelter them?

Tom decided immediately, if he couldn't help Plantain's sister, who could he help? He could borrow a single bed from a neighbor, place it alongside his, and use the couch and a folding cot for the twins. The housing director and his neighbor agreed to this temporary setup.

When he reached Barbara in Ohio, she cried. She was so grateful and at her wits end. He wired $300 from his savings for bus tickets and food, and instructed her to call him about their estimated arrival time at the Port Authority bus terminal in New York so he could meet them.

At the terminal, their only bag was placed on the curb. Tom bought tickets for New London. They were famished, and had to wait an hour, so he fed them with hot dogs from a vendor. While eating, he looked them over: the twins, a boy and a girl, were clean, but Barbara was a sore sight with bruises, a splint on her arm, and a somnolent appearance from exhaustion. By the unusual manner she begged for another hot dog, Tom realized that she had lost her feminine dignity and was really troubled.

On the bus, the twins fell asleep and they finally had a chance to talk. Tears ran down her cheek. "I married Bob because I wanted to stay near my folks and Dad commended him. But harvests were bad, our income fell, and we couldn't pay our bills. Bob became unhinged, told me to do more work, and blamed me if it wasn't done. After he beat me up, the hospital sent me to the shelter. I was so desperate when I wrote to you. Thanks, I'll always be grateful. I'll try to rebuild my life as fast as possible to get out of your hair."

14. Rebuilding

The day started with Tom being usually tranquil, but lots of excitement happened, making him somewhat giddy. Barbara reminded him of Jane in so many ways that he was glad to help. Tom was reassuring. Unburdened after her travails, suddenly she fell fast asleep.

When the bus stopped at the rest station in Darien, Connecticut, they used the facilities. The twins had never seen so many types of junk food before. Tom said, "One each!" He wasn't going to be their ruination. The rest of the ride was quiet; everyone slept. Then they took a taxi to Tom's apartment in Groton.

Barbara looked around, "It's tight, but we'll manage. Do you mind if I take a hot shower? I feel cruddy." Tom fed the kids oatmeal. She slept soundly for the first time in days until one of the twins woke her at noon. She emerged with an agency nightgown and asked, "We're about the same size. Can I wear one of your shirts and jeans?" Minutes later, she pranced about the living room, laughing, "How do I look? Do I still look like Mom?" Her twins thought Mom was hilarious. Barbara felt much better.

After eating, the reconstruction began. "Show me the laundry so I can wash our clothes?" Barbara said. Tom had a roll of quarters. The older guys in the complex went nuts over Tom's new friend and made fools of themselves. At 4 p.m., they had pizza on a table in the shady backyard. Neighbors introduced themselves. Afterward, he found a sitter and for relaxation took Barbara to a play at the Senior Center—she was spellbound. On Sunday, Tom hiked to Bluff Point with the twins, who had never seen the ocean before. The water was so calm that Bob Jr. asked, "Isn't it supposed to have waves?" On Monday, he took Barbara to Groton Family Services. Tom waited outside and then drove her to Goodwill to pick up clothes. Barbara said, "They gave me a food voucher, too, so let's do some grocery shopping." She cooked a simple meal. Tom took her to the nearby clinic where the splint was removed. She was okay.

"Tomorrow, I made an appointment for counseling. Can you watch the kids?" Tom's small savings were eroding, even with help from Family Services. So after the twins were asleep, he briefed Barbara. She didn't know what to do; her folks were gone and even if she initiated a divorce, she knew Bob couldn't pay alimony and child support. The agency advised her to apply for a job at Pfizer, Electric Boat, and the casinos. A day later, a female personnel manager at Pfizer took notice of her presence of mind, modest dress, quiet deportment, intelligence, and high school education and offered her an entry level job as a receptionist. The pay was modest, but provided important medical benefits. She arranged child care and while Tom babysat, began looking for an apartment in the older, less expensive, section of town. Barbara found a furnished third floor apartment owned by a widow. To Tom, it was dated, but she didn't mind. He didn't have enough money for the deposit. The widow understood Barbara's predicament, took a shine to her, and said she could make weekly payments until caught up. They made more trips to Goodwill.

In less than three weeks, enterprising Barbara had constructed a new life. Having her and the twins around was wonderful company for Tom and he would miss them, but his working days were over and his minimum disability payments could never support all of them. Tom was emotional on moving day, but both realized he had saved them. They were a link to his beloved Plantain. Barbara hugged him for a long time.

On the next Saturday morning, she called before visiting for two hours. She brought the donuts and he made coffee. Barbara knew Tom was lonely and looked forward to company. The visits developed into a regular weekend routine, a coffee klatch. Often, the landlady would join them.

During previous years, Tom found a walking partner for weekdays. Joe was a successful retiree and native, who loved their conversations so much that he continued them in his driveway. They walked together for years and never ran out of things to talk about. Joe was so elated about a good labs report that he bought a used convertible. Less than a week later, a blown tire caused a flipover. When he discussed the deaths of Joe and Jane with Barbara, they pondered, "Is it true, their time was up, or is it possible to buy extensions of life — with expensive medical treatments and organ transplants?"

Like many women, Barbara could read subliminal negative feelings in Tom's comments and gave him reasons to live with visits and calls. She kept the twins in Groton schools. "In ten years you'll be able to attend their graduations." He was pleased by her attention, always looking out for him. He wasn't that old, but was treated with respect, like a *paterfamilias*. He taught the twins how to play Rummy. They engaged him in their games.

It was so much fun. He played catch with them and when they were old enough, bought tickets to see the Sox.

Barbara relied on him when discipline was needed for her brood. He did it positively and firmly, and never yelled or browbeat them. They listened because of respect. Barbara taught them how to take care of themselves and insisted on compliance.

But when Tom visited his old landlord Jim and Kenny in Cranston, memories simply overwhelmed him. He had to stop visiting.

After her divorce, Barbara had several dates, but they were either gropers, drunks, or athletic nuts, watching game after game. All wanted sex on the first date. They might be bigger and taller, but none measured up to Tom's gentle behavior. Disillusioned, she stopped going out.

15. A Potpourri of Culture, Writing, and Tears

Tom had a small income and a shrinking attention span. Both hindered him when considering bus trips from the Senior Center. However, he managed to save enough to make two memorable bus trips to visit friends in the City. They took him to MoMA exhibitions: first by a sculptor and next, modern artists. Tom discovered Gustav Klimt, who worked in gold, and Tom researched his eccentric life back at the library.

Tom and another friend visited the Newport Playhouse. They attended experimental plays and student dance concerts at Conn College, becoming acquainted with department chairs. He invited Barbara and the twins to the semi-annual dance concert. They loved it so much that they asked to return for the spring function. In his own small way, he supported the arts in this very culture-rich area.

Before Barbara's arrival, his doctor suggested that Tom find a hobby—he had too much time on his hands. When Tom discussed possible activities with Bryan, his friend strongly recommended writing: "There's a writing group that meets at the library. Why don't you attend for several weeks? It might be the answer."

After several weeks, the members encouraged Tom to begin journaling, an expanded diary. Instead of just a few facts and dates, the process of expounding on a topic leads to questions, research, and possibly a story. Besides occupying his mind, it would assist his efforts in self-education.

Two months later, on a quarterly visit, Tom's doctor noticed the positive changes in his patient and insisted that he keep writing.

On Sundays, Tom went to Mass an hour early in the new chapel at St. Edmunds to pray for Plantain. Did God know her real name? He lit candles for Jane. It seemed like an ancient ritual; did these mystical methods work? He didn't know—but the short outburst of tears purged Tom of the day's sadness and melancholy. He blew his nose, welcomed friends, and during Mass, listened to the still valid wisdom of ancient biblical passages.

Tom was sad when he crossed off names in his notebook. It was extremely hard to find new friends to replace the old ones. And so, sorrow tinged his writing, until the Arts counteracted it. The area was so culture-rich that it generated many profound concepts.

16. Holidays

After age 55, Tom signed up for an exercise class at the Senior Center. He instituted his alternate-day, exercise regimen: walking to and inside the center, and participating in the exercise class.

In late November, six months after arriving, Barbara called, "What are you doing for Thanksgiving?"

"I usually go to a church in Mystic with friends."

She said, "I may be eligible for a free turkey—why don't you plan on eating with us?"

She didn't have to ask twice—Tom loved being with them and had such a good time that from that point on, every major holiday was spent with her family.

He marveled at the way Barbara maintained her dignity. She had a mission in life. Although dressed plainly, her personality showed through and attracted many friends, Tom would have been lost without Barbara.

17. Story: Revisions to Mindset

Six years after his walking partner died, Tom visited his niece's family in North Carolina. A classmate's wife suddenly died from a heart attack. Two more friends began treatments for prostate problems. Two had colorectal operations. Blindness threatened another.

Tom attended oceanographic lectures, poetry sessions, the symphony, movies, plays, and two cruises on Narragansett Bay. Other trips were entertaining but lacked the beauty of Chinese parasol dancing on a bus trip. Was it authentic? Regardless, it was riveting. They saw spectacular dance concerts and experimental theater at Conn College.

He broke two ribs in the dark bedroom, but recovered to become a docent for four hours on Sundays at a local museum. He escorted a friend to events. Few bought his books—most were given away or loaned. He opted out of mass publication. His taste and the public's were wildly out of sync.

He continued to revise older efforts and completed a few new works. Too bad the guts of the books weren't as colorful as the covers. His eyes tired easily and he sat too long. His decision to alternate writing with walking and reading, looked like a good one. It would complete his "tour of duty."

Then his oldest childhood friend died. Shocked by this turn of events, Tom worked faster, as if to thwart death. In Bristol, R.I., he saw immense Sequoias and Redwoods, which seduced him to live that long. A periodical from the AARP touted the increased age of each generation due to nutrition, medicines, treatments, exercise, and now gene repair.

The generation after Tom would average 100 years and the following 125 years! The maximum human lifespan was 155 years. Tom had grown to love life, but didn't want to live that long—maybe 100? His health was better than all his friends. He had found the proper mixture of exercise, work, social life and solitude.

His cousin ordered him to live to 105.

What did gene repair mean? It was incomprehensible for his donkey brain. However, gene repair promised to cure genetic cancers and myriad other ailments. It would result in a Nobel Prize for researchers, and give science fiction writers a brand new field. But would the end result be "designer babies" like Barbie doll? Could humans act like God? He knew the rich would try it. Who would care for mistakes?

Was 100 possible? Could his life continue that long? Plenty of time was available for revisions to previous work;

He didn't have to rush. Slowdown and enjoy life.

Tom did that and had the best month since Plantain's death.

18. Conclusion

A clear distinction exists between solitude and loneliness: the joy and pain of being alone. Solitude is a state of isolation (lack of contact with people). Complete isolation causes sensory deprivation. However, this can be avoided by keeping one's mind (and body) busy. Many see long-term solitude as undesirable, leading to clinical depression. But monks have produced spiritual enlightenment for centuries.

In *The Handbook of Solitude*, R. Coplan and J. Bowker disagree that solitude is dysfunctional and undesirable, noting that solitude can enhance self-esteem, clarity, and be therapeutic. Positive effects include freedom, increased creativity, the development of self, increased contemplation and spirituality. And loneliness can be avoided with (periodic) relations with others. However, prison solitude isn't beneficial. Negative effects also depend on age, particularly elementary children or teenagers.

Solitude can be a source of pleasure. The repetition of the Catholic Rosary brings supplicants into prayerful grace. The Buddha meditated to attain enlightenment. However, Introverted individuals may have to recharge in society.

**

TV had brainwashed Tom's relatives about the need for electronic toys and cruises. They never visited. For years, he had heaped praise on them, yet now they seemed ashamed of Tom.

In *Four Quartets*, T.S. Eliot wrote,

"Go, Go, Go, said the bird: Human kind cannot bear very much reality."

Even though he had refused to abandon his sickly parents, and now continued to escort an elderly friend, infrequent phone calls were his lot.

John Donne warned: "No man is an island, entire of itself;"

Tom wondered if mainstream American life was dissolving into small electronic islands, with "pride going before a big fall."

Did Eliot foresee it in *Four Quartets*?

"Shall I say it again? In order to arrive there,
To arrive where you are, to get from where you are not, You must go by a way wherein there is no ecstasy."

November, 2010, was one of Tom's best all-around months. Lots of writing, solitude and socialization happened. Was it the beginning of a new life? Groton was simply marvelous, much better than other towns. The surrounding area provided almost all of the activities, restaurants, shopping, and services that seniors crave. Tom and a friend patronized cultural events.

He read; researched with the help of librarians; wrote for long hours; exercised or walked; ate simple meals and nutritious lunches. Expensive cruises were ignored. Even inexpensive day trips were dropped. When Barbara and the kids visited, it was so pleasant and satisfying that it felt like the family he had lost. Year by year, he was getting better.

Thoreau and the Quakers were correct. Simple living was great.

19. The Rising Tide of Optimism

Since 2000, Tom had called Army and Cranston buddies, and checked on other contacts. He wished these links with old friends and new neighbors alleviated some of the loneliness and led to a successful retirement, but only two friends call; relatives never! They undoubtedly won't. However, Barbara's family was a godsend—He looked forward to their calls and visits.

A thorough reading of Tom's poems showed that improvements in self-esteem were uneven. But each year, advice from Barbara, friends, and physicians jogged his personality higher until finally reaching higher ground in 2010. Tom can walk to the Senior Center or Library in eight minutes. As he walked inside the Center, his joints loosened and while striding down the long back corridor, he remembered Barbara's friendly instruction, "Don't slouch—Stand tall!"

During the year, he made new friends by saying "Good Morning" to everyone. The seniors all knew his name though he didn't know theirs. Sometimes, his conversations alternated between happy members of two successive exercise groups.

The social aspect of exercise is unheralded. Tom ate lunch in the cafeteria with a man who nearly died in a motorcycle accident. The meal cost $4.75 and kept them going. Both agreed that nutrition, exercise, and socialization were positive factors in a senior's life and wondered why more didn't take advantage of them?

Tom's written observations are nowhere near the enthusiasm and optimism felt within. His doctor remarked, "You're doing fine." One of Tom's positive poems was "*Optimism, 2016.*"

Poem: Optimism, 2016

Before Thanksgiving, Tom's more optimistic,
Than he's been in a long time.

In life, from a shocked husband,
To a wearied retiree.

And now, a busy hobbyist,
Whose poems don't compete with pros.

And deliberately, his books lack violence,
He's content with new friends.

Director gave his pride a nudge,
Librarians have been invaluable.

Sure his health isn't perfect,
but whose is?

As Mary Oliver wrote in *Wild Geese*,
"Tell me about despair, yours,
and I will tell you mine."

He doesn't know when
this wonderful life will close
He doesn't remember when it opened.

But Tom had a lovable wife, her sister's care,
A girlfriend, a perceptive "Angel," and solid friends.

Let's stop talking about our ailments,
And talk about life!

In his stories, Tom drastically reduced repetition, held firm those of ordinary people; and except for the Quakers, kept most personal religious beliefs to himself. Boyhood and Army buddies, hikers, pretty women, current residents, Senior Center or Library personnel, writers, and relatives were considered, elsewhere.

Tom had rescued Barbara and her twins; now she watched out for him. It was almost like "déjà vu."

At first, he babysat, and a few years later, picked up the twins at the bus stop. Soon, Tom drove them for Soccer and Lacrosse. He began to discuss careers with the kids.

Tom encouraged higher education, and helped with scholarship and college applications. He attended their graduation in 2010.

As bright students from a low-income family, several colleges offered free tuition with work-study for expenses. After reading the offers, Barbara gave Tom the biggest hug ever. They both cried—they had done it! He was justifiably proud.

Tom never forgot his "Plantain" and helped her sister whenever asked. Even though his income was limited, he had done all he could. Barbara and he would remain friends, forever. Wise Ben Franklin reportedly said "It is better to be useful in life than rich."

Tom had been useful. He was at peace.

Sources:

Wikipedia

Milton Berle's Joke Book

Thoreau: *Walden; Walking; The Maine Woods; A Week on the Concord and...; Civil Disobedience; Life without Principle;*

The Night Thoreau Spent in Jail, R. Lee

Plain Living, Catherine Whitmire

American Heritage Dictionary of American Quotations

Finding a Way to Follow, W. Coleman

Four Quartets; the Waste Land, T.S. Eliot

Audubon Society Field Guides

Claire Carter (deceased cousin)

Eastern Connecticut Symphony Orchestra

Rhode Island Hospital

Groton Senior Center, and Groton Public Library

Stillness, R. Mahler

Connecticut College productions

AARP bulletin

The Handbook of Solitude, Coplan and Bowker

The Simplicity Collective

Medical News Today: Preeclampsia

History of Childbirth Deaths, L. Helmuth

When Your Time is Up, A. Wagstaff

Made in the USA
Columbia, SC
19 September 2022